The Penguin, evil as ever, has stolen the Warhawk, a powerful fighting machine with all the latest weapons. In his hands, it could mean doom – if Batman can't get it back...

British Library Cataloguing in Publication Data

Hatch, Constance V.
  The Warhawk.
  I. Title   II. Howarth, Walter   III. Series
  813'.54 [J]
  ISBN 0-7214-1234-3

First edition

Published by Ladybird Books Ltd Loughborough Leicestershire UK
Ladybird Books Inc Auburn Maine 04210 USA

Printed in England

BAT MAN
THE WARHAWK

by Constance V Hatch
illustrated by Walter Howarth

Ladybird Books

"It's the greatest advance we've ever made, Bruce," said Alan Lance, Chairman of the Board of Gotham Aircraft Company.

Bruce Wayne was impressed as he walked with his friend into what was probably the largest hangar ever built. In front of them was a tremendously long military plane unlike anything he had ever seen before. As Bruce and Alan stood at one end of it, they could barely see the other end of the plane. It was as big as that!

The last thing Bruce heard as he fell into a deep sleep was the Penguin mumbling to himself. "This is only the first step in my journey," said the villain. "The first step in the footsteps of Admiral Byrd!"

Bruce and Alan were dumped outside, then the gangplank rolled up into its place on the side of the plane.

Seconds later the villain was in the cockpit. The long roof of the hangar slid open automatically as he started the great engines of the *Warhawk*. The plane took off vertically through the opened roof, and with one burst of speed, it was gone.

When Bruce and Alan at last woke up on the floor of the hangar, Alan said anxiously, "There were nuclear weapons aboard that plane. How are we going to get it back?"

Bruce began to make his way back to his private limousine. "I think I know someone who can help you," he told Alan before Alfred, his butler and trusted friend, took him back to Wayne Manor.

When they arrived, Alfred drove Bruce straight into the secret cavern that led to an even more mysterious place, the Bat Cave. Here, Bruce changed into his caped outfit, becoming that powerful avenger of the night, Batman!

"Will you need the Batmobile, sir?" asked Alfred. He was one of the few men alive who knew his master's twin identities.

"Not this time, Alfred. It will have to be the Batplane. Only the Batplane is fast enough to keep up with the *Warhawk*."

"Surely the Penguin didn't tell you where he was going to take the plane?" asked Alfred, puzzled.

Batman grinned. "Oh, but he did! Before the gas knocked me out, the Penguin said he was going to follow in the footsteps of Admiral Byrd – who was famous for his expedition to Antarctica."

"So that's where he's taking the *Warhawk*! I must say, very clever, sir," said Alfred admiringly.

Batman climbed into the Batplane and took off. For just one moment the plane's silhouette could be seen high up against the clouds, then it disappeared.

It was not long before Batman was over the Antarctic and gazing down at the huge bleak continent. He thought, "He won't hide from me! His plane will leave a trail of heat, and I can follow it on my infra-red screen."

Sure enough, he soon found the *Warhawk*. Batman landed his plane some distance away behind a huge snowbank, and set out to trudge his way through the deep, deep snow.

As he neared the *Warhawk*, Batman slowed down. In front of him was a huge fortress, something like a medieval castle, carved out of ice. What could it be?

After a moment, he went slowly and carefully through the gate and suddenly heard a chuckle. His arch-enemy was in the courtyard, feeding hundreds of his pet birds. Some were in heated cages, and others were flying freely around the icy towers of the Penguin's home base.

Luckily the villain had his back to the entrance, and Batman managed to hide quickly. The Penguin was talking happily to his birds. "You think this place is a bird sanctuary, my feathered friends," said the

Penguin. "But soon – very soon – it will be quite a different kind of sanctuary!"

Interested, Batman tried to move closer to hear properly.

"Soon this whole continent of Antarctica will be mine," boasted the villain. "I'll rule it myself. There'll be no police… and no prisons! It's going to be a sanctuary for criminals who will pay me good money to keep them safe from the police of every country in the world. Once they are here, no one will be able to arrest them."

"So that's his plan," thought Batman, edging still closer. "Worst of all, the Penguin's new country will have nuclear weapons. He could easily start a third World War! I've got to get the *Warhawk* back to Gotham!"

Batman crept out through the gate and ran to the stupendous plane, hoping to pilot it back home. He touched the switch for the gangplank – but it had been booby-trapped! A chirping siren went off, and a set of bars dropped neatly over Batman.

The Penguin turned up instantly, to give Batman yet another blast of the knockout gas! Once more, the Caped Crusader was out cold.

When he came to, Batman was lying on a sheet of ice. His arms and legs were each tied to a wooden stake, driven deep in the ice. Above him there was a huge slope with an overhanging cliff at the top.

He turned his head to see the Penguin standing nearby. All round the villain were cages filled with birds. The Penguin started to hook up microphones to every cage. "All these mikes are connected to a giant sound amplifier," he said. "Pretty soon, I'm going to rattle the cages of these warblers, and they'll start to sing like crazy. There'll be so much noise from the amplifier that it will cause an

avalanche, bringing down tons of snow and ice from that cliff just above you. I'll be far away," he chortled, "but you'll be buried, Batman!"

True to his word, the Penguin went to each cage and shook it. The birds began to twitter, and suddenly, there seemed to be hundreds upon hundreds of chattering birds!

The din was unbelievable! As the Penguin went back to his castle chuckling, another noise started. There was a slow rumble as the ice from the cliff above began to crack and shatter. Batman could see that the wall of the cliff was beginning to split. Soon huge boulders of ice would tumble down upon him, spelling his doom.

He had to do something quickly. He managed to grab one of the wooden stakes that held him down, and used his tremendous strength to break it. This gave him one hand free, and he reached into his utility belt for a Batarang. Aiming it carefully, he tossed it straight at the wires that connected the microphones to the amplifier. With a hail of fizzling sparks, the chattering of the birds died away.

When the Batarang came back to him, Batman caught it one-handed. He knew that he had no time to lose, and working as fast as he could, he cut the rest of his bonds. Then, brushing the snow off his cape, he sped to the *Warhawk*.

This time, he used the Batarang to short-circuit the booby-trapped gangplank, and

the stairs unfolded so that he could climb
into the plane. But at the top, there was the
Penguin, pointing his umbrella straight at
Batman's face.

Once more, the ugly green gas escaped
from the parasol's tip. "That won't work this
time, Penguin," said Batman. "I'm using the
anti-gas nose filters from my utility belt."

The Penguin swung round and raced for the cockpit. "Not so fast," said Batman. He took a small net from his belt and tossed it straight at his foe. The net expanded, completely covering the Penguin, and no matter how hard he tried, he could not get free. He was Batman's prisoner.

"You're not getting the *Warhawk*, Penguin! It's too dangerous for any government to use, let alone one with you in charge," said Batman. "You can sing like those birds of yours to a judge, then you're going behind bars where you belong."

The Penguin opened his mouth to speak, but his reply went unheard as the engines of the *Warhawk* revved up to take the giant plane back to its hangar in Gotham City.